W9-CJW-316

The
ENCHANTED
TAPESTRY

A Chinese folktale retold by
Robert D. San Souci

pictures by
László Gál

Dial Books for Young Readers / New York

57479

SHENENDEHOWA PUBLIC LIBRARY
47 CLIFTON COUNTRY ROAD
CLIFTON PARK, NEW YORK 12065

Published by Dial Books for Young Readers
2 Park Avenue
New York, New York 10016

Text copyright © 1987 by Robert D. San Souci
Pictures copyright © 1987 by László Gál
All rights reserved
Design by Atha Tehon
Printed in Hong Kong by South China Printing Co.
First edition
W
2 4 6 8 10 9 7 5 3 1

Library of Congress Cataloging-in-Publication Data
San Souci, Robert.
The Enchanted Tapestry.
Summary: With the aid of a sorceress, young Li Ju
seeks his mother's precious handmade tapestry held
by the fairies of Sun Mountain.
[1. Fairy tales. 2. Folklore—China.]
I. Gál, László, ill. II. Title.
PZ8.S248En 1987   398.2′1′0951 [E]   85-29283
ISBN 0-8037-0304-X
ISBN 0-8037-0306-6 (lib. bdg.)

The full-color artwork was prepared using watercolor
washes, gouache, and colored pencils.
It was then color-separated and reproduced
as red, blue, yellow, and black halftones.

For my parents
Robert Abraham San Souci
Mary Ellen San Souci
Once again, with love

R.S.S.

For Philip and Rose Quan

L.G.

A long time ago a widow lived in a small house near a forest in China. Like her grandmother and mother, she made her living by weaving tapestry.

Her skillful fingers turned silk yarns of every color into flowers, trees, birds, animals, even people—each was a work of art. Her tapestries always brought the highest prices, and she was able to raise her three sons—Li Mo, Li Tu, and Li Ju—on the gold people paid for her handi-work. Some people proudly hung her largest pieces on their walls; while those who could only afford smaller samples of her work made them into beautiful waistcoats or bedspreads.

One day she began to weave a picture of a fine house with lovely flower gardens, trees, and peaceful green fields surrounding it. The image caught her fancy. She worked on it day after day, month after month. She added a footbridge arching gracefully over a gentle stream and rich green meadows that swept up toward towering mountains.

On and on she worked, adding new details.

Her eldest son, Li Mo, and her middle son, Li Tu, tried to make her stop working on the tapestry.

"We have sold all the other tapestries," grumbled Li Mo. "How are we supposed to live if you don't give us anything to sell?"

"There's little food left in the house," added Li Tu, "and even less money."

But the old woman stayed at her loom, working by sunlight and candlelight. When tears came to her eyes from strain, she wove them into a fish pond brimming with sleek goldfish; when she pricked her finger with a splinter, she wove the drops of blood into brilliant red

flowers and a glowing sun like a huge lantern above the mountains.

"There's no money to buy rice," muttered Li Mo.

And Li Tu said, "We're all going to starve."

But their mother replied, "I must finish this piece of tapestry."

Finally the youngest son, Li Ju, became a woodcutter, earning just enough to buy rice for them all. His brothers complained that he made barely enough to keep them alive and urged him to work harder. Because he was so good-natured, Li Ju merely sighed and tried to cut even more wood than before.

After more than a year the old woman said, "I am nearly finished. A few more days will complete my tapestry."

"Mother, it's beautiful," said Li Ju, gazing at the grand house with white walls, blue-tile roof, and huge front doors of red. It stood in a garden of rainbow-colored flowers.

"That piece of tapestry will bring us lots of money," said Li Mo, rubbing his hands together.

"Hurry and finish it," urged Li Tu, "so we can sell it and never again have only rice to eat and patched clothes to wear."

The old woman said nothing, but went on with her work.

The next morning, at sunrise, she wove the likeness of herself, standing at the door of the house, into the tapestry scene.

Li Ju, watching said, "Mother, this tapestry is your dream, isn't it?"
She nodded.

"You must never sell it," her youngest son told her.

She smiled as she silently wove into the tapestry the image of Li Ju standing at her side.

Suddenly Li Mo bustled into the room and cried, "Aren't you done yet? Hurry and finish so we can sell this."

Li Tu, who had followed him in, said, "Don't waste time adding more.

It will bring a high price the way it is." He reached for the tapestry, saying,
"Let us turn this into good food and fine clothes right away." But his
mother would not let him touch it.

Then she said, "This tapestry is a picture of everything I hold dear in my dreams and in my life. All my children should be in it, but I haven't had time to put you there."

"What does it matter?" asked Li Mo. "We're hungry."

"And ashamed of our patched clothes," added Li Tu.

"We only want the gold this will bring," they said together.

"Finish it the way you want," said Li Ju quietly to his mother.

His two brothers began yelling at him, and their mother was forced to turn from her loom to make peace.

Suddenly a gusty wind blew in through the western window, ripped the tapestry from its frame, and whirled it away out the eastern window.

They all pursued it, but it swirled away into the distance and vanished.

The old woman fainted. Li Ju carried her back into the house and gently put her on the bed. Li Mo and Li Tu wept on each other's shoulders because of the fortune that had been snatched away from them.

When she had recovered enough to speak, the widow called her eldest son to her bedside and said, "Li Mo, go to the East and find my tapestry, or I will die."

Grumbling, Li Mo set out and traveled east.

After a month he came to a mountain pass, where he found a stone hut with a stone horse standing in front of it. A white-haired old woman leaned out of the hut's single window and asked, "Where are you going, young man?"

Li Mo told her what had happened.

"That tapestry was taken by the fairies of Sun Mountain in the East," said the old woman, who was really a powerful sorceress. "They love beautiful things, but they will return it, if you ask.

"However, it is very difficult to get there. First you have to cut your finger and place ten drops of blood on my stone horse's flank so he can move. Then you must ride him through the flame mountains. His magic will protect you most of the time, except when you go through the fire. There you must not make a sound. If you utter a cry or show any fear, you will be burned to ashes.

"Then you must cross a sea of freezing waves filled with jagged ice and lashed by terrible winds. My horse will take you safely much of the way. But if you complain once, or even shiver, you will turn to ice and sink to the bottom of the sea.

"Beyond its farthest shore, you will find Sun Mountain and your mother's tapestry."

Li Mo hesitated, thinking of blood and fire and ice.

The sorceress laughed and said, "If this frightens you, take this gold instead." And she held out to him a bag filled with gold coins.

Li Mo grabbed it eagerly, then ran away to the city to spend it on himself.

The old widow grew even more sickly.

When Li Mo didn't come back, she said to her middle son, "Li Tu, bring back my tapestry or I will certainly die."

With much complaining, Li Tu set out along the eastern road. After a month's journey he met the sorceress in the stone hut at the mountain pass.

But when she told him the things he would have to do to get back the tapestry, he, too, took the gold she offered and hurried off to the city to spend it on himself.

The old mother grew thin as a dried reed. Finally her youngest son, Li Ju, came to her and said, "Let me go and search for the tapestry."

At first she did not want to let him go, because her other sons had disappeared. But he insisted, and at last she let him go with her blessing.

Li Ju was so eager to save his mother's life that it took him only half a month to reach the hut with the stone horse in front.

The sorceress told him what he had to do, then offered Li Ju her gold. But he answered, "No, I must fetch my mother's tapestry, or she will die."

So he followed the old woman's instructions and ten drops of his blood fell on the stone horse. It came to life with a whinny, shook out its silky

mane, and stamped its hooves, eager to begin their journey. Li Ju leaped
on its back, grasping its mane, and they galloped away to the East.

Soon they came to the flaming moutains and the icy sea. Though the
heat of the mountains blistered Li Ju's face, he made no sound and let
himself show no fear. The horse leaped from ice floe to ice floe across the
sea, while waves, lashed by freezing winds to a fury, threatened to drown
them. But Li Ju did not allow himself the tiniest shiver.

And so they passed through in safety.

On the farthest shore, they came to Sun Mountain. Halfway up was a palace built of gold. Beautiful fairies dressed in rainbow silks gathered on the broad steps, staring in wonder at the human who had risked such dangers to reach them.

The most beautiful one of all, dressed in red, came down to meet Li Ju. She greeted him, then introduced him to her sisters.

When he told them why he had come, the one in red said, "We are bound to return the tapestry to you. But you cannot cross to mortal lands at night. Rest, and I will bring you the tapestry in the morning."

Tired out from his adventures, Li Ju agreed, and soon fell asleep on a couch they showed him.

But the red-robed fairy had fallen in love with the young man. While her sisters slept, she hung a huge, glowing pearl on a rafter and spent the night weaving a picture of herself and part of her magic into the wonderful tapestry.

The next morning Li Ju took the carefully folded tapestry the fairy gave to him. He thanked her and tucked it inside his shirt, next to his heart.

Then he galloped back across the icy sea and through the flaming mountains. Soon he returned in safety to the stone hut beside the mountain pass. There he returned the horse to the sorceress, and it became stone once again.

"Hurry, young man," said the old woman, "your mother is dying."

Li Ju ran night and day to where his mother lay wasting away.

"Mother! Mother!" he cried, bursting into her room, "I've brought your tapestry back!"

He pinned it to the wall for her to see; eagerly she raised herself up out of her bed, already feeling her health returning.

A ray of morning sunlight suddenly struck the tapestry through the eastern window.

The cloth began to grow and grow, until it covered the whole wall.

It grew even more, and soon it became a landscape into which mother and son could step.

Together they walked toward the magnificent house with white walls, blue-tile roof, and proud red doors that lay before them. They crossed a lovely footbridge over a stream filled with shining water; they paused to exclaim over a fishpond filled with sleek goldfish. Gentle breezes from the distant mountains rippled the meadow grass and made blossoms of every imaginable color bow as Li Ju and his mother passed by.

And, waiting at the front door, her dress as red as the doors themselves and the great red sun overhead, was the beautiful fairy.

As it happened, Li Ju married the beautiful fairy, and the three of them—mother, son, wife—lived very happily together.

One evening, two beggars (who were really Li Mo and Li Tu, after spending all their gold) came to the gates of the grand house. They saw their mother, brother, and a graceful woman in red strolling in the gardens.

But when the brothers tried to push open the gate, a whirlwind rose up, blinding them for a moment with flying dirt and spinning them around.

When the windstorm ceased, Li Mo and Li Tu found themselves on a strange road in an unfamiliar place. Each was holding a piece of faded and tattered tapestry, while faint, mocking laughter came to their ears from far away in the East.